The Jameson Satellite

The Jameson Satellite
Neil R. Jones

ÆGYPAN PRESS

Special thanks to Greg Weeks, Stephen Blundell, and the
Online Distributed Proofreading Team (which can be found
at http://www.pgdp.net).

This text was first published in *Amazing Stories*, July, 1931.

The Jameson Satellite
A publication of
ÆGYPAN PRESS

www.aegypan.com

The mammoths of the ancient world have been wonderfully preserved in the ice of Siberia. The cold, only a few miles out in space, will be far more intense than in the polar regions and its power of preserving the dead body would most probably be correspondingly increased. When the hero-scientist of this story knew he must die, he conceived a brilliant idea for the preservation of his body, the result of which even exceeded his expectations. What, how, and why are cleverly told here.

Prologue

The Rocket Satellite

*I*n the depths of space, some twenty thousand miles from the earth, the body of Professor Jameson within its rocket container cruised upon an endless journey, circling the gigantic sphere. The rocket was a satellite of the huge, revolving world around which it held to its orbit. In the year 1958, Professor Jameson had sought for a plan whereby he might preserve his body indefinitely after his death. He had worked long and hard upon the subject.

Since the time of the Pharaohs, the human race had looked for a means by which the dead might be preserved against the ravages of time. Great had been the art of the Egyptians in the embalming of their deceased, a practice which was later lost to humanity of the ensuing mechanical age, never to be rediscovered. But even the embalming of the Egyptians — so Professor Jameson had argued — would be futile in the face of millions of years, the dissolution of the corpses being just as eventual as immediate cremation following death.

The professor had looked for a means by which the body could be preserved perfectly forever. But eventually he had come to the conclusion that nothing on earth is unchangeable beyond a certain limit of time. Just as long as he sought an earthly means of preservation, he was doomed to disappointment. All earthly elements are composed of atoms which are forever breaking down and building up, but never destroying themselves. A match may be burned, but the atoms are still unchanged, having resolved themselves into smoke, carbon dioxide, ashes, and certain basic elements. It was clear to the professor that he could never accomplish his purpose if he were to employ one system of atomic structure, such as embalming fluid or other concoction, to preserve another system of atomic structure, such as the human body, when all atomic structure is subject to universal change, no matter how slow.

He had then soliloquized upon the possibility of preserving the human body in its state of death until the end of all earthly time — to that day when the earth would return to the sun from which it had sprung. Quite suddenly one day he had conceived the answer to the puzzling problem which obsessed his mind, leaving him awed with its wild, uncanny potentialities.

He would have his body shot into space enclosed in a rocket to become a satellite of the earth as long as the earth continued to exist. He reasoned logically. Any material substance, whether of organic or inorganic origin, cast into the depths of space would exist indefinitely. He had visualized his dead body enclosed in a rocket flying off into the illimitable maw of space. He would remain in perfect preservation, while on earth millions of generations of mankind would live and die, their bodies to molder into the dust of the forgotten past. He would exist in this unchanged manner until that day when mankind, beneath a cooling sun, should fade out forever in the chill, thin atmosphere of a dying world. And still his body would remain intact and as perfect in its rocket container as on that day of the far-gone past when it had left the earth to be hurled out on its career. What a magnificent idea!

At first he had been assailed with doubts. Suppose his funeral rocket landed upon some other planet or, drawn by the pull of the great sun, were thrown into the flaming folds of the incandescent sphere? Then the rocket might continue on out of the solar system, plunging through the endless seas of space for millions of years, to finally enter the solar system of some far-off star, as meteors often enter ours. Suppose his rocket crashed upon a planet, or the star itself, or became a captive satellite of some celestial body?

It had been at this juncture that the idea of his rocket becoming the satellite of the earth had presented itself, and he had immediately incorporated it into his scheme. The professor had figured out the amount of radium necessary to carry the rocket far enough away from the earth so that it would not turn around and crash, and still be not so far away but what the earth's gravitational attraction would keep it from leaving the vicinity of the earth and the solar system. Like the moon, it would forever revolve around the earth.

He had chosen an orbit sixty-five thousand miles from the earth for his rocket to follow. The only fears he had entertained concerned the huge meteors which careened through space at tremendous rates of speed. He had overcome this obstacle, however, and had eliminated the possibilities of a collision with these stellar juggernauts. In the rocket were installed radium repulsion rays which swerved all approaching meteors from the path of the rocket as they entered the vicinity of the space wanderer.

The aged professor had prepared for every contingency, and had set down to rest from his labors, reveling in the stupendous, unparalleled results he would obtain. Never would his body undergo decay; and never would his bones bleach to return to the dust of the earth from which all men originally came and to which they must return. His body would remain millions of years in a perfectly preserved state, untouched by the hoary palm of such time as only geologists and astronomers can conceive.

His efforts would surpass even the wildest dreams of H. Rider Haggard, who depicted the wondrous, embalming practices of the ancient nation of Kor in his immortal novel, "She," wherein Holly, under the escort of the incomparable Ayesha, looked upon the magnificent, lifelike masterpieces of embalming by the long-gone peoples of Kor.

With the able assistance of a nephew, who carried out his instructions and wishes following his death, Professor Jameson was sent upon his pilgrimage into space within the rocket he himself had built. The nephew and heir kept the secret forever locked in his heart.

Generation after generation had passed upon its way. Gradually humanity had come to die out, finally disappearing from the earth altogether. Mankind was later replaced by various other forms of life which dominated the globe for their allotted spaces of time before they too became extinct. The years piled up on one another, running into millions, and still the Jameson Satellite kept its lonely vigil around the earth, gradually closing the distance between satellite and planet, yielding reluctantly to the latter's powerful attraction.

Forty million years later, its orbit ranged some twenty thousand miles from the earth while the dead world edged ever nearer the cooling sun whose dull, red ball covered a large expanse of the sky. Surrounding the flaming sphere, many of the stars could be perceived through the earth's thin, rarefied atmosphere. As the earth cut in slowly and gradually toward the solar luminary, so was the moon revolving ever nearer the earth, appearing like a great gem glowing in the twilight sky.

The rocket containing the remains of Professor Jameson continued its endless travel around the great ball of the earth whose rotation had now ceased entirely — one side forever facing the dying sun. There it pursued its lonely way, a cosmic coffin, accompanied by its funeral cortege of scintillating stars amid the deep silence of the eternal space which enshrouded it. Solitary it remained, except for the occasional passing of a meteor flitting by at a remarkable speed on its aimless journey through the vacuum between the far-flung worlds.

Would the satellite follow its orbit to the world's end, or would its supply of radium soon exhaust itself after so many eons of time, converting the rocket into the prey of the first large meteor which chanced that way? Would it some day return to the earth as its nearer approach portended, and increase its acceleration in a long arc to crash upon the surface of the dead planet? And when the rocket terminated its career, would the body of Professor Jameson be found perfectly preserved or merely a crumbled mound of dust?

Chapter I

40,000,000 Years After

*E*ntering within the boundaries of the solar system, a long, dark, pointed craft sped across the realms of space towards the tiny point of light which marked the dull red ball of the dying sun which would some day lie cold and dark forever. Like a huge meteor it flashed into the solar system from another chain of planets far out in the illimitable Universe of stars and worlds, heading towards the great red sun at an inconceivable speed.

Within the interior of the space traveler, queer creatures of metal labored at the controls of the space flyer which juggernauted on its way towards the far-off solar luminary. Rapidly it crossed the orbits of Neptune and Uranus and headed sunward. The bodies of these queer creatures were square blocks of a metal closely resembling steel, while for appendages, the metal cube was upheld by four jointed legs capable of movement. A set of six tentacles, all metal, like the rest of the body, curved outward from the upper half of the cubic body. Surmounting it was a queer-shaped head rising to a peak in the center and equipped with a circle of eyes all the way around the head. The creatures, with their mechanical eyes equipped with metal shutters, could see in all directions. A single eye pointed directly upward, being situated in the space of the peaked head, resting in a slight depression of the cranium.

These were the Zoromes of the planet Zor which rotated on its way around a star millions of light years distant from our solar system. The Zoromes, several hundred thousand years before, had reached a stage in science, where they searched for immortality and eternal relief from bodily ills and various deficiencies of flesh and blood anatomy. They had sought freedom from death, and had found it, but at the same time they had destroyed the propensities for birth. And for several hundred thousand years there had been no births and few deaths in the history of the Zoromes.

This strange race of people had built their own mechanical bodies, and by operation upon one another had removed their brains to the metal heads from which they directed the functions and movements of their inorganic anatomies. There had been no deaths due to worn-out bodies. When one part of the mechanical men wore out, it was replaced by a new part, and so the Zoromes continued living their immortal lives which saw few casualties. It was true that, since the innovation of the machines, there had been a few accidents which had seen the destruction of the metal heads with their brains. These were irreparable. Such cases had been few, however, and the population of Zor had decreased but little. The machine men of Zor had no use for atmosphere, and had it not been for the terrible coldness of space, could have just as well existed in the ether void as upon some planet. Their metal bodies, especially their metal-encased brains, did require a certain amount of heat even though they were able to exist comfortably in temperatures which would instantly have frozen to death a flesh-and-blood creature.

The most popular pastime among the machine men of Zor was the exploration of the Universe. This afforded them a never ending source of interest in the discovery of the variegated inhabitants and conditions of the various planets on which they came to rest. Hundreds of space ships were sent out in all directions, many of them being upon their expeditions for hundreds of years before they returned once more to the home planet of far-off Zor.

This particular space craft of the Zoromes had entered the solar system whose planets were gradually circling in closer to the dull red ball of the declining sun. Several of the machine men of the space craft's crew, which numbered some fifty individuals, were examining the various planets of this particular planetary system carefully through telescopes possessing immense power.

These machine men had no names and were indexed according to letters and numbers. They conversed by means of thought impulses, and were neither capable of making a sound vocally nor of hearing one uttered.

"Where shall we go?" queried one of the men at the controls questioning another who stood by his side examining a chart on the wall.

"They all appear to be dead worlds, 4R-3579," replied the one addressed, "but the second planet from the sun appears to have an atmosphere which might sustain a few living creatures, and the third planet may also prove interesting for it has a satellite. We shall examine the inner planets first of all, and explore the outer ones later if we decide it is worth the time."

"Too much trouble for nothing," ventured 9G-721. "This system of planets offers us little but what we have seen many times before in our travels. The sun is so cooled that it cannot sustain the more common life on its planets, the type of life forms we usually find in our travels. We should have visited a planetary system with a brighter sun."

"You speak of common life," remarked 25X-987. "What of the uncommon life? Have we not found life existent on cold, dead planets with no sunlight and atmosphere at all?"

"Yes, we have," admitted 9G-721, "but such occasions are exceedingly rare."

"The possibility exists, however, even in this case," reminded 4R-3579, "and what if we do spend a bit of unprofitable time in this one planetary system — haven't we all an endless lifetime before us? Eternity is ours."

"We shall visit the second planet first of all," directed 25X-987, who was in charge of this particular expedition of the Zoromes, "and on the way there we shall cruise along near the third planet to see what we can of the surface. We may be able to tell whether or not it holds anything of interest to us. If it does, after visiting the second planet, we shall then return to the third. The first world is not worth bothering with."

*T*he space ship from Zor raced on in a direction which would take it several thousand miles above the earth and then on to the planet which we know as Venus. As the space ship rapidly neared the earth, it slackened its speed, so that the Zoromes might examine it closely with their glasses as the ship passed the third planet.

Suddenly, one of the machine men ran excitedly into the room where 25X-987 stood watching the topography of the world beneath him.

"We have found something!" he exclaimed.

"What?"

"Another space ship!"

"Where?"

"But a short distance ahead of us on our course. Come into the foreport of the ship and you can pick it up with the glass."

"Which is the way it's going?" asked 25X-987.

"It is behaving queerly," replied the machine man of Zor. "It appears to be in the act of circling the planet."

"Do you suppose that there really is life on that dead world — intelligent beings like ourselves, and that this is one of their space craft?"

"Perhaps it is another exploration craft like our own from some other world," was the suggestion.

"But not of ours," said 25X-987.

Together, the two Zoromes now hastened into the observation room of the space ship where more of the machine men were excitedly examining the mysterious space craft, their thought impulses flying thick and fast like bodiless bullets.

"It is very small!"

"Its speed is slow!"

"The craft can hold but few men," observed one.

"We do not yet know of what size the creatures are," reminded another. "Perhaps there are thousands of them in that space craft out there. They may be of such a small size that it will be necessary to look twice before finding one of them. Such beings are not unknown."

"We shall soon overtake it and see."

"I wonder if they have seen us?"

"Where do you suppose it came from?"

"From the world beneath us," was the suggestion.

"Perhaps."

Chapter II

The Mysterious Space Craft

*T*he machine men made way for their leader, 25X-987, who regarded the space craft ahead of them critically.

"Have you tried communicating with it yet?" he asked.

"There is no reply to any of our signals," came the answer.

"Come alongside of it then," ordered their commander. "It is small enough to be brought inside our carrying compartment, and we can see with our penetration rays just what manner of creatures it holds. They are intelligent, that is certain, for their space ship does imply as much."

The space flyer of the Zoromes slowed up as it approached the mysterious wanderer of the cosmic void which hovered in the vicinity of the dying world.

"What a queer shape it has," remarked 25X-987. "It is even smaller than I had previously calculated."

A rare occurrence had taken place among the machine men of Zor. They were overcome by a great curiosity which they could not allow to remain unsatiated. Accustomed as they were to witnessing strange sights and still stranger creatures, meeting up with weird adventures in various corners of the Universe, they had now become hardened to the usual run of experiences which they were in the habit of encountering. It took a great deal to arouse their unperturbed attitudes. Something new, however, about this queer space craft had gripped their imaginations, and perhaps a subconscious influence asserted to their minds that here they have come across an adventure radically unusual.

"Come alongside it," repeated 25X-987 to the operator as he returned to the control room and gazed through the side of the space ship in the direction of the smaller cosmic wanderer.

"I'm trying to," replied the machine man, "but it seems to jump away a bit every time I get within a certain distance of it. Our ship seems to jump backward a bit too."

"Are they trying to elude us?"

"I don't know. They should pick up more speed if that is their object."

"Perhaps they are now progressing at their maximum speed and cannot increase their acceleration any more."

"Look!" exclaimed the operator. "Did you just see that? The thing has jumped away from us again!"

"Our ship moved also," said 25X-987. "I saw a flash of light shoot from the side of the other craft as it jumped."

Another machine man now entered and spoke to the commander of the Zorome expedition.

"They are using radium repellent rays to keep us from approaching," he informed.

"Counteract it," instructed 25X-987.

The man left, and now the machine man at the controls of the craft tried again to close with the mysterious wanderer of the space between planets. The effort was successful, and this time there was no glow of repulsion rays from the side of the long metal cylinder.

They now entered the compartment where various objects were transferred from out the depths of space to the interplanetary craft. Then patiently they waited for the rest of the machine men to open the side of their space ship and bring in the queer, elongated cylinder.

"Put it under the penetration ray!" ordered 25X-987. "Then we shall see what it contains!"

The entire group of Zoromes were assembled about the long cylinder, whose low nickel-plated sides shone brilliantly. With interest they regarded the fifteen-foot object which tapered a bit towards its base. The nose was pointed like a bullet. Eight cylindrical protuberances were affixed to the base while the four sides were equipped with fins such as are seen on aërial bombs to guide them in a direct, unswerving line through the atmosphere. At the base of the strange craft there projected a lever, while in one side was a door which, apparently opened outward. One of the machine men reached forward to open it but was halted by the admonition of the commander.

"Do not open it up yet!" he warned. "We are not aware of what it contains!"

Guided by the hand of one of the machine men, a series of lights shone down upon the cylinder. It became enveloped in a haze of light which rendered the metal sides of the mysterious space craft dim and indistinct while the interior of the cylinder was as clearly revealed as if there had been no covering. The machine men, expecting to see at least several, perhaps many, strange creatures moving about within the metal cylinder, stared aghast at the sight they beheld. There was but one creature, and he was lying perfectly still, either in a state of suspended animation or else of death. He was about twice the height of the mechanical men of Zor. For a long time they gazed at him in a silence of thought, and then their leader instructed them.

"Take him out of the container."

The penetration rays were turned off, and two of the machine men stepped eagerly forward and opened the door. One of them peered within at the recumbent body of the weird-looking individual with the four appendages. The creature lay up against a luxuriously upholstered interior, a strap affixed to his chin while four more straps held both the upper and lower appendages securely to the insides of the cylinder. The machine man released these, and with the help of his comrade removed the body of the creature from the cosmic coffin in which they had found it.

"He is dead!" pronounced one of the machine men after a long and careful examination of the corpse. "He has been like this for a long time."

"There are strange thought impressions left upon his mind," remarked another.

One of the machine men, whose metal body was of a different shade than that of his companions, stepped forward, his cubic body bent over that of the strange, cold creature who was garbed in fantastic accoutrements. He examined the dead organism a moment, and then he turned to his companions.

"Would you like to hear his story?" he asked.

"Yes!" came the concerted reply.

"You shall, then," was the ultimatum. "Bring him into my laboratory. I shall remove his brain and stimulate the cells into activity once more. We shall give him life again, transplanting his brain into the head of one of our machines."

With these words he directed two of the Zoromes to carry the corpse into the laboratory.

As the space ship cruised about in the vicinity of this third planet which 25X-987 had decided to visit on finding the metal cylinder with its queer inhabitant,

8B-52, the experimenter, worked unceasingly in his laboratory to revive the long-dead brain cells to action once more. Finally, after consummating his desires and having his efforts crowned with success, he placed the brain within the head of a machine. The brain was brought to consciousness. The creature's body was discarded after the all-important brain had been removed.

Chapter III

Recalled to Life

*A*s Professor Jameson came to, he became aware of a strange feeling. He was sick. The doctors had not expected him to live; they had frankly told him so — but he had cared little in view of the long, happy years stretched out behind him. Perhaps he was not to die yet. He wondered how long he had slept. How strange he felt — as if he had no body. Why couldn't he open his eyes? He tried very hard. A mist swam before him. His eyes had been open all the time but he had not seen before. That was queer, he ruminated. All was silent about his bedside. Had all the doctors and nurses left him to sleep — or to die?

Devil take that mist which now swam before him, obscuring everything in line of vision. He would call his nephew. Vainly he attempted to shout the word "Douglas," but to no avail. Where was his mouth? It seemed as if he had none. Was it all delirium? The strange silence — perhaps he had lost his sense of hearing along with his ability to speak — and he could see nothing distinctly. The mist had transferred itself into a confused jumble of indistinct objects, some of which moved about before him.

He was now conscious of some impulse in his mind which kept questioning him as to how he felt. He was conscious of other strange ideas which seemed to be impressed upon his brain, but this one thought concerning his indisposition clamored insistently over the lesser ideas. It even seemed just as if someone was addressing him, and impulsively he attempted to utter a sound and tell them how queer he felt. It seemed as if speech had been taken from him. He could not talk, no matter how hard he tried. It was no use. Strange to say, however, the impulse within his mind appeared to be satisfied with the effort, and it now put another question to him. Where was he from? What a strange question — when he was at home. He told them as much. Had he always lived there? Why, yes, of course.

The aged professor was now becoming more astute as to his condition. At first it was only a mild, passive wonderment at his helplessness and the strange thoughts which raced through his mind. Now he attempted to arouse himself from the lethargy.

Quite suddenly his sight cleared, and what a surprise! He could see all the way around him without moving his head! And he could look at the ceiling of his room! His room? Was it his room! No — It just couldn't be. Where was he? What were those queer machines before him? They moved on four legs. Six tentacles curled outward from their cubical bodies. One of the machines stood close before him. A tentacle shot out from the object and rubbed his head. How strange it felt upon his brow. Instinctively he obeyed the impulse to shove the contraption of metal from him with his hands.

His arms did not rise, instead six tentacles projected upward to force back the machine. Professor Jameson gasped mentally in surprise as he gazed at the result of his urge to push the strange, unearthly looking machine-caricature from him. With trepidation he looked down at his own body to see where the tentacles had come from, and his surprise turned to sheer fright and amazement. His body was like the moving machine which stood before him! Where was he? What ever had happened to him so suddenly? Only a few moments ago he had been in his bed, with the doctors and his nephew bending over him, expecting him to die. The last words he had remembered hearing was the cryptic announcement of one of the doctors.

"He is going now."

But he hadn't died after all, apparently. A horrible thought struck him! Was this the life after death? Or was it an illusion of the mind? He became aware that the machine in front of him was attempting to communicate something to him. How could it, thought the professor, when he had no mouth. The desire to communicate an idea to him became more insistent. The suggestion of the machine man's question was in his mind. Telepathy, thought he.

The creature was asking about the place whence he had come. He didn't know; his mind was in such a turmoil of thoughts and conflicting ideas. He allowed himself to be led to a window where the machine with waving tentacle pointed towards an object outside. It was a queer sensation to be walking on the four metal legs. He looked from the window and he saw that which caused him to nearly drop over, so astounded was he.

The professor found himself gazing out from the boundless depths of space across the cosmic void to where a huge planet lay quiet. Now he was sure it was an illusion which made his mind and sight behave so queerly. He was troubled by a very strange dream. Carefully he examined the topography of the gigantic globe which rested off in the distance. At the same time he could see back of him the concourse of mechanical creatures crowding up behind him, and he was aware of a telepathic conversation which was being carried on behind him — or just before him. Which was it now? Eyes extended all the way around his head, while there existed no difference on any of the four sides of his cubed body. His mechanical legs were capable of moving in any of four given directions with perfect ease, he discovered.

The planet was not the earth — of that he was sure. None of the familiar continents lay before his eyes. And then he saw the great dull red ball of the dying sun. That was not the sun of his earth. It had been a great deal more brilliant.

"Did you come from that planet?" came the thought impulse from the mechanism by his side.

"No," he returned.

He then allowed the machine men — for he assumed that they were machine men, and he reasoned that, somehow or other they had by some marvelous transformation made him over just as they were — to lead him through the craft of which he now took notice for the first time. It was an interplanetary flyer, or space ship, he firmly believed.

25X-987 now took him to the compartment which they had removed him to from the strange container they had found wandering in the vicinity of the nearby world. There they showed him the long cylinder.

"It's my rocket satellite!" exclaimed Professor Jameson to himself, though in reality every one of the machine men received his thoughts plainly. "What is it doing here?"

"We found your dead body within it," answered 25X-987. "Your brain was removed to the machine after having been stimulated into activity once more. Your carcass was thrown away."

Professor Jameson just stood dumfounded by the words of the machine man.

"So I did die!" exclaimed the professor. "And my body was placed within the rocket to remain in everlasting preservation until the end of all earthly time! Success! I have now attained unrivaled success!"

He then turned to the machine man.

"How long have I been that way?" he asked excitedly.

"How should we know?" replied the Zorome. "We picked up your rocket only a short time ago, which, according to your computation, would be less than a day. This is our first visit to your planetary system and we chanced upon your rocket. So it is a satellite? We didn't watch it long enough to discover whether or not it was a satellite. At first we thought it to be another traveling space craft, but when it refused to answer our signals we investigated."

"And so that was the earth at which I looked," mused the professor. "No wonder I didn't recognize it. The topography has changed so much. How different the sun appears — it must have been over a million years ago when I died!"

"Many millions," corrected 25X-987. "Suns of such size as this one do not cool in so short a time as you suggest."

Professor Jameson, in spite of all his amazing computations before his death, was staggered by the reality.

"Who are you?" he suddenly asked.

"We are the Zoromes from Zor, a planet of a sun far across the Universe."

25X-987 then went on to tell Professor Jameson something about how the Zoromes had attained their high stage of development and had instantly put a stop to all birth, evolution and death of their people, by becoming machine men.

Chapter IV

The Dying World

"And now tell us of yourself," said 25X-987, "and about your world."

Professor Jameson, noted in college as a lecturer of no mean ability and perfectly capable of relating intelligently to them the story of the earth's history, evolution and march of events following the birth of civilization up until the time when he died, began his story. The mental speech hampered him for a time, but he soon became accustomed to it so as to use it easily, and he found it preferable to vocal speech after a while.

The Zoromes listened interestedly to the long account until Professor Jameson had finished.

"My nephew," concluded the professor, "evidently obeyed my instructions and placed my body in the rocket I had built, shooting it out into space where I became the satellite of the earth for these many millions of years."

"Do you really want to know how long you were dead before we found you?" asked 25X-987. "It would be interesting to find out."

"Yes, I should like very much to know," replied the professor.

"Our greatest mathematician, 459C-79, will tell it to you." The mathematician stepped forward. Upon one side of his cube were many buttons arranged in long columns and squares.

"What is your unit of measuring?" he asked.

"A mile."

"How many times more is a mile than is the length of your rocket satellite?"

"My rocket is fifteen feet long. A mile is five thousand two hundred and eighty feet."

The mathematician depressed a few buttons.

"How far, or how many miles from the sun was your planet at that time?"

"Ninety-three million miles," was the reply.

"And your world's satellite — which you call moon from your planet — earth?"

"Two hundred and forty thousand miles."

"And your rocket?"

"I figured it to go about sixty-five thousand miles from the earth."

"It was only twenty thousand miles from the earth when we picked it up," said the mathematician, depressing a few more buttons. "The moon and sun are also much nearer your planet now."

*P*rofessor Jameson gave way to a mental ejaculation of amazement.

"Do you know how long you have cruised around the planet in your own satellite?" said the mathematician. "Since you began that journey, the planet which you call the earth has revolved around the sun over forty million times."

"Forty — million — years!" exclaimed Professor Jameson haltingly. "Humanity must then have all perished from the earth long ago! I'm the last man on earth!"

"It is a dead world now," interjected 25X-987.

"Of course," elucidated the mathematician, "those last few million years are much shorter than the ones in which you lived. The earth's orbit is of less diameter and its speed of revolution is greatly increased, due to its proximity to the cooling sun. I should say that your year was some four times as long as the time in which it now takes your old planet to circumnavigate the sun.

"How many days were there in your year?"

"Three hundred and sixty-five."

"The planet has now ceased rotating entirely."

"Seems queer that your rocket satellite should avoid the meteors so long," observed 459C-79, the mathematician.

"Automatic radium repulsion rays," explained the professor.

"The very rays which kept us from approaching your rocket," stated 25X-987, "until we neutralized them."

"You died and were shot out into space long before any life occurred on Zor," soliloquized one of the machine men. "Our people had not yet even been born when yours had probably disappeared entirely from the face of the earth."

"Hearken to 72N-4783," said 25X-987, "he is our philosopher, and he just loves to dwell on the past life of Zor when we were flesh and blood creatures with the threat of death hanging always over our heads. At that time, like the life you knew, we were born, we lived and died, all within a very short time, comparatively."

"Of course, time has come to mean nothing to us, especially when we are out in space," observed 72N-4783. "We never keep track of it on our expeditions, though back in Zor such accounts are accurately kept. By the way, do you know how long we stood here while you recounted to us the history of your planet? Our machine bodies never get tired, you know."

"Well," ruminated Professor Jameson, giving a generous allowance of time. "I should say about a half a day, although it seemed scarcely as long as that."

"We listened to you for four days," replied 72N-4783.

Professor Jameson was really aghast.

"Really, I hadn't meant to be such a bore," he apologized.

"That is nothing," replied the other. "Your story was interesting, and if it had been twice as long, it would not have mattered, nor would it have seemed any longer. Time is merely relative, and in space actual time does not exist at all, anymore than your forty million years' cessation of life seemed more than a few moments to you. We saw that it was so when your first thought impressions reached us following your revival."

"Let us continue on to your planet earth," then said 25X-987. "Perhaps we shall find more startling disclosures there."

As the space ship of the Zoromes approached the sphere from which Professor Jameson had been hurled in his rocket forty million years before, the professor was wondering how the earth would appear, and what radical changes he would find. Already he knew that the geographical conditions of the various continents were changed. He had seen as much from the space ship.

A short time later the earth was reached. The space travelers from Zor, as well as Professor Jameson, emerged from the cosmic flyer to walk upon the surface of the planet. The earth had ceased rotating, leaving one-half its surface always toward the sun. This side of the earth was heated to a considerable degree, while its antipodes, turned always away from the solar luminary, was a cold, frigid, desolate waste. The space travelers from Zor did not dare to advance very far into either hemisphere, but landed on the narrow, thousand-mile strip of territory separating the earth's frozen half from its sun-baked antipodes.

As Professor Jameson emerged from the space ship with 25X-987, he stared in awe at the great transformation four hundred thousand centuries had wrought. The earth's surface, its sky and the sun were all so changed and unearthly appearing. Off to the east the blood red ball of the slowly cooling sun rested upon the horizon, lighting up the eternal day. The earth's rotation had ceased entirely, and it hung motionless in the sky as it revolved around its solar parent, its orbit slowly but surely cutting in toward the great body of the sun. The two inner planets, Mercury and Venus, were now very close to the blood red orb whose scintillating, dazzling brilliance had been lost in its cooling process. Soon, the two nearer planets would succumb to the great pull of the solar luminary and return to the flaming folds, from which they had been hurled out as gaseous bodies in the dim, age-old past, when their careers had just begun.

The atmosphere was nearly gone, so rarefied had it become, and through it Professor Jameson could view with amazing clarity without discomfort to his eyes the bloated body of the dying sun. It appeared many times the size he had seen it at the time of his death, on account of its relative nearness. The earth had advanced a great deal closer to the great star around which it swung.

The sky towards the west was pitch black except for the iridescent twinkle of the fiery stars which studded that section of the heavens. As he watched, a faint glow suffused the western sky, gradually growing brighter, the full moon majestically lifted itself above the horizon, casting its pale, ethereal radiance upon the dying world beneath. It was increased to many times the size Professor Jameson had ever seen it during his natural lifetime. The earth's greater attraction was drawing upon the moon just as the sun was pulling the earth ever nearer itself.

This cheerless landscape confronting the professor represented the state of existence to which the earth had come. It was a magnificent spread of loneliness which bore no witness to the fact that it had seen the teeming of life in better ages long ago. The weird, yet beautiful scene, spread in a melancholy panorama before his eyes, drove his thoughts into gloomy abstraction with its dismal, depressing influence. Its funereal, oppressive aspect smote him suddenly with the chill of a terrible loneliness.

25X-987 aroused Professor Jameson from his lethargic reverie. "Let us walk around and see what we can find. I can understand how you feel in regard to the past. It is quite a shock — but it must happen to all worlds sooner or later — even to Zor. When that time comes, the Zoromes will find a new planet on which to live. If you travel with us, you will become accustomed to the sight of seeing dead, lifeless worlds as well as new and beautiful ones pulsating with life and energy. Of course, this world being your own, holds a peculiar sentimental value to you, but it is really one planet among billions."

Professor Jameson was silent.

"I wonder whether or not there are any ruins here to be found?" queried 25X-987.

"I don't believe so," replied the professor. "I remember hearing an eminent scientist of my day state that, given fifty thousand years, every structure and other creation of man would be obliterated entirely from off the earth's surface."

"And he was right," endorsed the machine man of Zor. "Time is a great effacer."

For a long time the machine men wandered over the dreary surface of the earth, and then 25X-987 suggested a change of territory to explore. In the space ship, they moved around the earth to the other side, still keeping to the belt of shadowland which completely encircled the globe like some gigantic ring. Where they now landed arose a series of cones with hollow peaks.

"Volcanoes!" exclaimed the professor.

"Extinct ones," added the machine man.

Leaving the space ship, the fifty or more machine men, including also Professor Jameson, were soon exploring the curiously shaped peaks. The professor, in his wanderings had strayed away from the rest, and now advanced into one of the cuplike depressions of the peak, out of sight of his companions, the Zoromes.

Chapter V

Eternity or Death

*H*e was well in the center of the cavity when the soft ground beneath him gave way suddenly and he catapulted below into the darkness. Through the Stygian gloom he fell in what seemed to be an endless drop. He finally crashed upon something hard. The thin crust of the volcano's mouth had broken through, precipitating him into the deep, hollow interior.

It must have been a long ways to fall — or so it had seemed. Why was he not knocked senseless or killed? Then he felt himself over with three tentacles. His metal legs were four broken, twisted masses of metal, while the lower half of his cubic body was jammed out of shape and split. He could not move, and half of his six tentacles were paralyzed.

How would he ever get out of there? he wondered. The machine men of Zor might never find him. What would happen to him, then? He would remain in this deathless, monotonous state forever in the black hole of the volcano's interior unable to move. What a horrible thought! He could not starve to death; eating was unknown among the Zoromes, the machines requiring no food. He could not even commit suicide. The only way for him to die would be to smash the strong metal head, and in his present immovable condition, this was impossible.

It suddenly occurred to him to radiate thoughts for help. Would the Zoromes receive his messages? He wondered how far the telepathic messages would carry. He concentrated the powers of his mind upon the call for help, and repeatedly stated his position and plight. He then left his mind clear to receive the thought answers of the Zoromes. He received none. Again he tried. Still he received no welcoming answer. Professor Jameson became dejected.

*I*t was hopeless. The telepathic messages had not reached the machine men of Zor. They were too far away, just as one person may be out of earshot of another's voice. He was doomed to a terrible fate of existence! It were better that his rocket had never been found. He wished that the Zoromes had destroyed him instead of bringing him back to life — back to this!

His thoughts were suddenly broken in upon.

"We're coming!"

"Don't give up hope!"

If the professor's machine body had been equipped with a heart, it would have sung for joy at these welcome thought impressions. A short time later there appeared in the ragged break of the volcano's mouth, where he had fallen through, the metal head of one of the machine men.

"We shall have you out of there soon," he said.

*T*he professor never knew how they managed it for he lost consciousness under some strange ray of light they projected down upon him in his prison. When he came to consciousness once more, it was to find himself inside the space ship.

"If you had fallen and had smashed your head, it would have been all over with you," were the first thought impulses which greeted him. "As it is, however, we can fix you up first rate."

"Why didn't you answer the first time I called to you?" asked the professor. "Didn't you hear me?"

"We heard you, and we answered, but you didn't hear us. You see, your brain is different than ours, and though you can send thought waves as far as we can you cannot receive them from such a great distance."

"I'm wrecked," said the professor, gazing at his twisted limbs, paralyzed tentacles and jammed body.

"We shall repair you," came the reply. "It is your good fortune that your head was not crushed."

"What are you going to do with me?" queried the professor. "Will you remove my brains to another machine?"

"No, it isn't necessary. We shall merely remove your head and place it upon another machine body."

The Zoromes immediately set to work upon the task, and soon had Professor Jameson's metal head removed from the machine which he had wrecked in his fall down the crater. All during the painless operation, the professor kept up a series of thought exchanges in conversation with the Zoromes, and it seemed but a short time before his head surmounted a new machine and he was ready for further exploration. In the course of his operation, the space ship had moved to a new position, and now as they emerged 25X-987 kept company with Professor Jameson.

"I must keep an eye on you," he said. "You will be getting into more trouble before you get accustomed to the metal bodies."

But Professor Jameson was doing a great deal of thinking. Doubtlessly, these strange machine men who had picked up his rocket in the depths of space and had brought him back to life, were expecting him to travel with them and become adopted into the ranks of the Zoromes. Did he want to go with them? He couldn't decide. He had forgotten that the machine men could read his innermost thoughts.

"You wish to remain here alone upon the earth?" asked 25X-987. "It is your privilege if you really want it so."

"I don't know," replied Professor Jameson truthfully.

*H*e gazed at the dust around his feet. It had probably been the composition of men, and had changed from time to time into various other atomic structures — of other queer forms of life which had succeeded mankind. It was the law of the atom which never died. And now he had within his power perpetual existence. He could be immortal if he wished! It would be an immortality of never-ending adventures in the vast, endless Universe among the galaxy of stars and planets.

A great loneliness seized him. Would he be happy among these machine men of another far-off world — among these Zoromes? They were kindly and solicitous of his welfare. What better fate could he expect? Still, a longing for his own kind arose in him — the call of humanity. It was irresistible. What could he do? Was it not in vain? Humanity had long since disappeared from the earth — millions of years ago. He wondered what lay beyond the pales of death — the real death, where the body decomposed and wasted away to return to the dust of the earth and assume new atomic structures.

He had begun to wonder whether or not he had been dead all these forty millions of years — suppose he had been merely in a state of suspended animation.

He had remembered a scientist of his day, who had claimed that the body does not die at the point of official death. According to the claims of this man, the cells of the body did not die at the moment at which respiration, heart beats and the blood circulation ceased, but it existed in the semblance of life for several days afterward, especially in the cells of the bones, which died last of all.

Perhaps when he had been sent out into space in his rocket right after his death, the action of the cosmic void was to halt his slow death of the cells in his body, and hold him in suspended animation during the ensuing millions of years. Suppose he should really die — destroying his own brain? What lay beyond real death? Would it be a better plane of existence than the Zoromes could offer him? Would he rediscover humanity, or had they long since arisen to higher planes of existence or reincarnation? Did time exist beyond the mysterious portals of death? If not, then it was possible for him to join the souls of the human race. Had he really been dead all this time? If so, he knew what to expect in case he really destroyed his own brain. Oblivion!

Again the intense feeling of loneliness surged over him and held him within its melancholy grasp.

Desperately, he decided to find the nearest cliff and jump from it — head-first! Humanity called; no man lived to companion him. His four metal limbs carried him swiftly to the summit of a nearby precipice. Why not gamble on the hereafter? 25X-987, understanding his trend of thought, did not attempt to restrain him. Instead, the machine man of Zor waited patiently.

As Professor Jameson stood there meditating upon the jump which would hurl him now into a new plane of existence — or into oblivion, the thought transference of 25X-987 reached him. It was laden with the wisdom born of many planets and thousands of centuries' experience.

"Why jump?" asked the machine man. "The dying world holds your imagination within a morbid clutch. It is all a matter of mental condition. Free your mind of this fascinating influence and come with us to visit other worlds, many of them are both beautiful and new. You will then feel a great difference.

"Will you come?"

The professor considered for a moment as he resisted the impulse to dive off the declivity to the enticing rocks far below. An inspiration seized him. Backing away from the edge of the cliff, he joined 25X-987 once more.

"I shall come," he stated.

He would become an immortal after all and join the Zoromes in their never-ending adventures from world to world. They hastened to the space ship to escape the depressing, dreary influence of the dying world, which had nearly driven Professor Jameson to take the fatal leap to oblivion.

THE END